Vinnie in France® is published by

Pageturner Books®

THE LAUGH & LEARN TRAVEL SERIES

P.O. Box 171, Vineburg, California 95487

Published in 2001 by Pageturner Books
Text: © 2001 Elizabeth Bott
Illustrations: © 2001 Guido Frosini and Alessandra Cecchetti

Summary: A crazy cat's adventures in France.

ISBN 0-9704678-1-8

• FIRST EDITION •

Printed in the United States of America

Layout & Pre-press production by: Michael Hollyfield •Production Art • Sonoma

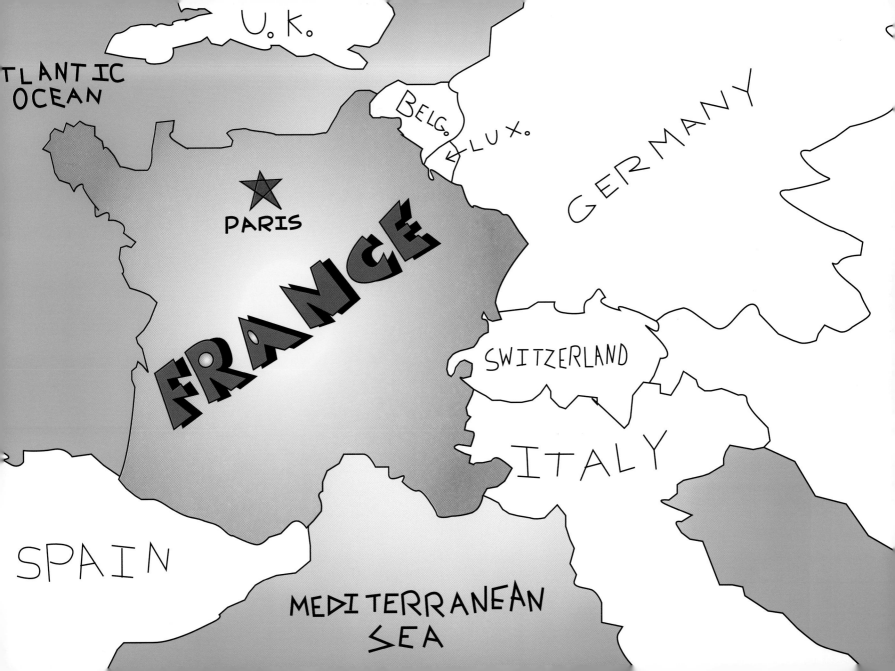

Dedicated to
Zia Ione, who taught us strength and courage.

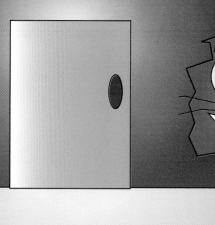

Oo la la, Vive la France! Hot croissants!

An American in Paris, the capital of France.

Standing on a street corner at an outdoor café,
Vinnie hailed a cab parked five blocks away.

Two cabbies took off at neck-breaking speed,
One swerved and turned, and took the lead.

A tire blew! He skidded and dented the hood.
Then he screeched to a halt where Vinnie stood.

"Bonjour, Monsieur," the driver said, "I'm Jean-Pierre.
My price is reasonable, my rates are fair."

"Leave it to me , I'm your driving tour guide!"
Vinnie wiggled his brows and jumped inside.

"To the Moulin Rouge for the dancing show
Where they serve champagne and escargot.

I'll teach you our language and history today.
Unless you already know how to 'parlez-français'?"

Vinnie shrugged, "Oui, oui . . . Fi Fi, poo poo, pee pee.
I am very bilingual as you can see."

They screamed with laughter and sped down the street
Singing French songs and stomping their feet.

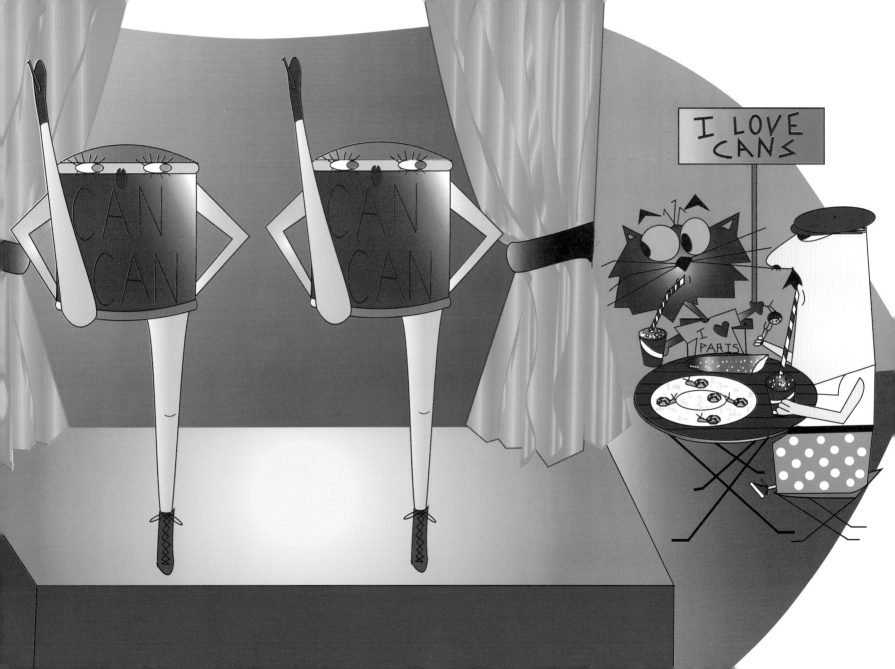

At the Moulin Rouge at a table for two
They ordered their food from a special menu.

Where Toulouse-Lautrec, famed artist of France
Painted ladies performing the cancan dance.

Their dinner was served as the dancing began.
And at once Vinnie became an instant fan.

"I love your country! Your food and your show!
I love your champagne and this escargot."

"I am happy you like our drink and snails.
It is French cuisine that never fails."

"Snails!" Vinnie jumped up, banging his chair.,
Gagging and spitting his food in the air.

"I thought it was chicken that I was to try.
I'd rather have hot pokers stuck in my eye."

"Please, Monsieur, you must stay calm and take care,
But your food has landed in some woman's hair!

Do not panic, Monsieur, she's coming this way.
Try to think of something complimentary to say."

"Madame," Vinnie said, "snails look great in your hair.
They bring out your highlights, they give you such flair."

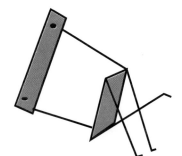

"It's you!" she screamed, tripping over a chair.
Her wig sailed off and flew through the air.

Vinnie leaped for the catch before hitting the floor,
Grabbed Jean-Pierre and ran out the back door.

"Buckle up, Monsieur, we are ready to move.
It's time we visited the museum of the Louvre."

They pulled up in front with the police all around.
"They are looking for someone who cannot be found.

Mon Dieu! Monsieur, you must wear a disguise.
They are looking for a cat with blue-colored eyes.

With the wig and sunglasses you are sure to get in.
I will tell them you are my American twin."

WANTED
IF FOUND CAII
1-800-GOT-CAT

Passing the guards they snuck in with the crowd,
Kept a low profile and tried not to be loud.

"There are thousands of objects of art to see
Including the statue, 'Winged Victory'.

A woman with wings without any head
Sculpted in marble, not bronze nor lead."

But it was da Vinci's most famous painting
That set Vinnie off to ranting and raving.

"Mona Lisa!" he shouted, "a woman of mystery
With the most famous smile in all of history.

Just look at that smile, that secretive glance.
My heart is beating with love and romance.

I know it is strange, it is only a painting.
But I am light-headed, I feel like fainting."

"That isn't love," said Jean-Pierre, "that wig is too tight.
It's numbing your head and affecting your sight."

Pulling it off Vinnie threw it to the floor.
"We'll need a diversion to get out the door."

Vinnie kicked it to the bald woman wearing a hat,
And then Vinnie shouted, "Look out for that rat!"

Lifting her purse up high over her head
The woman struck it until it was dead.

Vinnie screamed, "Run for your life, Jean-Pierre,
Before she finds out she's killed her own hair."

"Jump in the car and I'll show you the city,
To miss seeing Paris would be a great pity.

Look across the River Seine and you will see
A small model Statue of Liberty."

Jean-Pierre explained, "Fédéric Bartholdi designed two.
One statue for France and another for you."

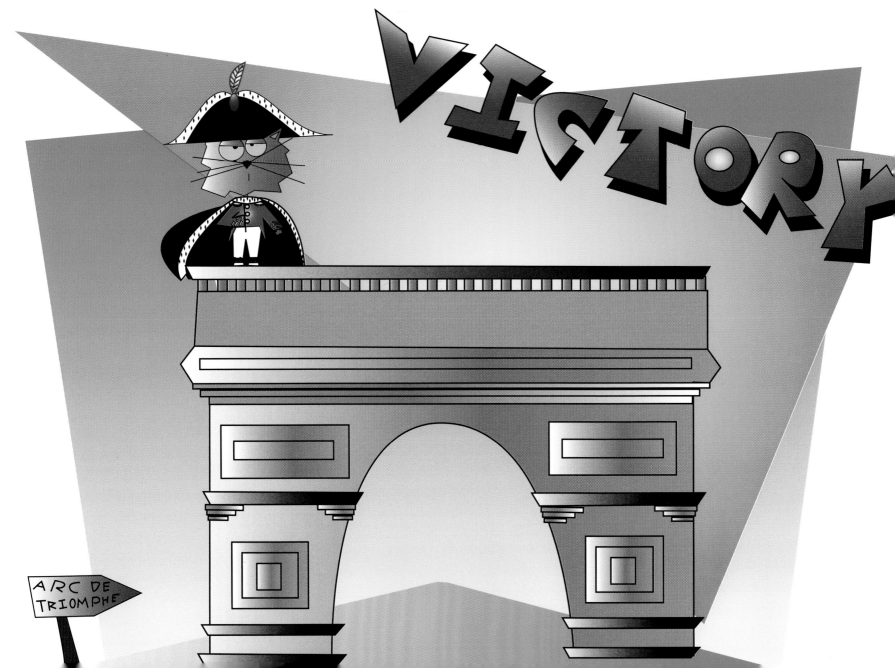

They drove down the Boulevard Champs-Elysées
To see the Arc de Triomphe in the light of day.

Honoring Napoleon's years of success
And the unknown soldier's place of rest.

"Napoleon was a famous emperor of France.
Not to be judged by the length of his pants.

He invaded Spain, Austria, Russia, too.
And was defeated in battle at Waterloo.

He wished to rule Europe and got people riled.
He caused so much trouble he was finally exiled."

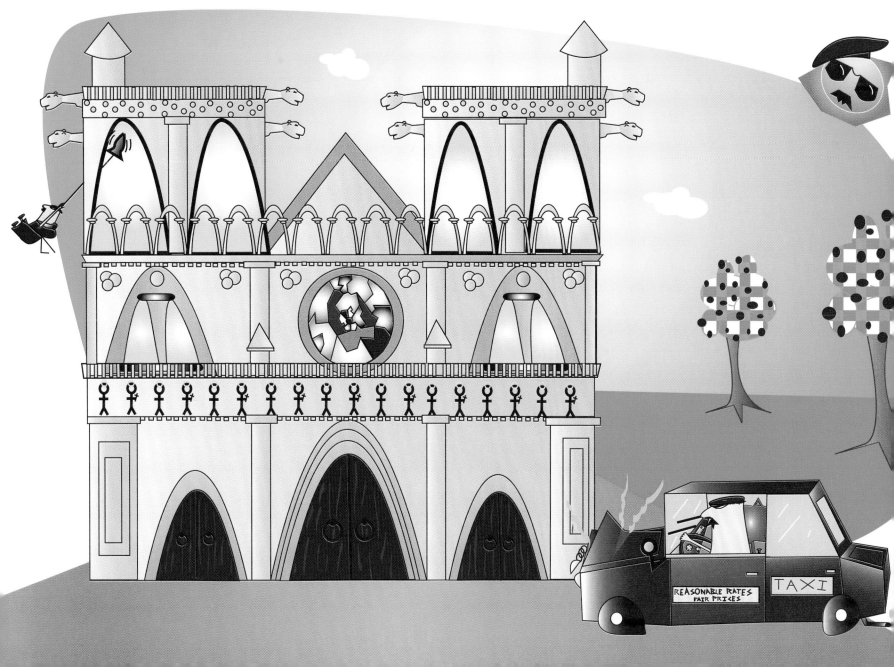

"Now to the Eiffel Tower," said Jean-Pierre,
    "Built for the 1889 World's Fair.

Next you will see where stone gargoyles perch.
They decorate the roof of the Notre Dame church.

It is one of the most famous cathedrals in town
Where kings and queens were ceremoniously crowned.

In a novel, Victor Hugo wrote of this place
About a man with a hump and an ugly face."

"Tragic heroes are a part of the history of France,
Like Joan of Arc who wore French armored pants.

She led the French army for the king's sake.
Captured by the English, she was burned at the stake."

"Jean-Pierre," Vinnie cried, "you are a wealth of knowledge.
Driving with you is like going to college."

"Oui, Monsieur, my stories are part of my trade.
But there are no papers to write, no tests, no grade."

" I'll make you a genius and teach you to paint.
They'll write books about you and make you a saint.

Our history is filled with intrigue and romance
From soldiers to artists to the rulers of France.

Good and bad kings have sat on the throne,
But Louis XIV and XVI are the most well known.

Louis the XIV built the palace of Versailles,
An enormous château that money can't buy.

Louis the XVI, the worst king of the time,
Stirred the French Revolution of 1789."

"The King and Queen were selfish and greedy.
While the peasants were starving, homeless and needy.

'Let them eat cake,' said Queen Marie Antoinette.
Famous last words that she would live to regret.

The peasants joined forces and finally revolted
King Louis and his Queen got scared and bolted.

They were soon recaptured and sent to prison.
They pleaded for mercy but no one would listen.

Condemned to death on the guillotines,
Louis' head came off and so did the Queen's."

With his eyes glazed over Vinnie sat in the back
Listening to Pierre give fact after fact.

"Monsieur Vinnie, you are getting that look
As if you've been reading a geometry book.

We will leave Paris by an old country road.
You suffer from something we call tour-overload.

To Arles, the home of painter Vincent van Gogh
Who died without knowing how famous he'd grow."

From Arles back to Paris they enjoyed the view.
When Pierre slammed on the brakes and yelled, "Mon Dieu!"

"Monsieur Vinnie, there is a roadblock ahead.
I will roll down my window to hear what is said.

They look for you, they say you're a pest.
They've hired a vet, who says he won't rest.

They've blocked the roads, the airport, too.
There is only one thing left for us to do."

"To the train station," Vinnie ordered Jean-Pierre.
"I will travel over land and not by air."

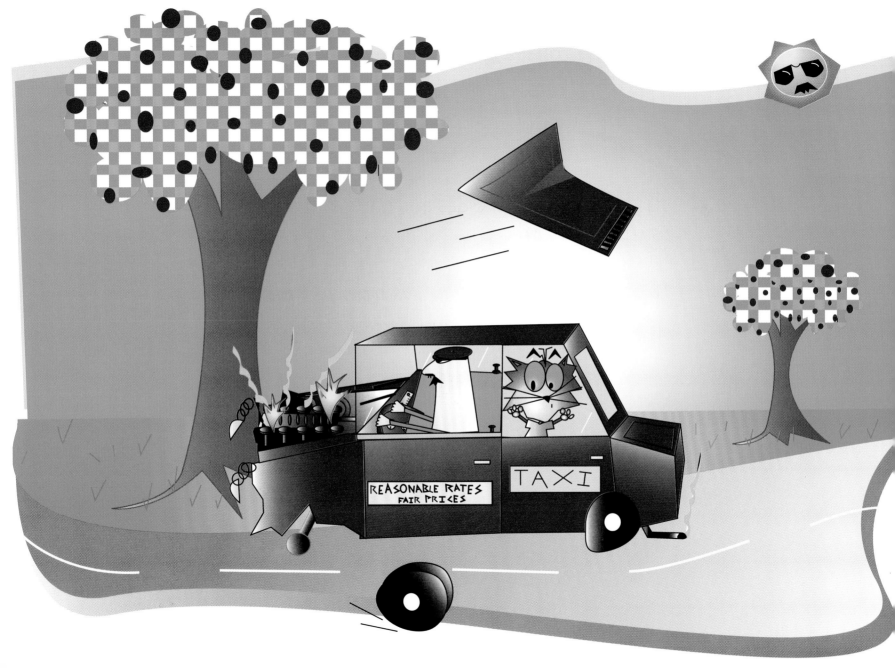

"Oui, Monsieur, I am your driving tour guide.
Buckle your belt and get ready to ride."

Jean-Pierre stepped on the gas and the car spun around.
Hitting a tree the hood fell to the ground.

"Do not worry, Monsieur, it is only a nick.
I am a good driver, I know every trick."

He drove over the hood, and lost the front tire.
Vinnie watched it roll by as the engine caught fire.

"Death is not an option for me, Jean-Pierre."
"Oui, oui, Monsieur, you've nothing to fear."

"Monsieur, I have good and bad news I need to share.
The station's not far, we are almost there."

"And what is the bad news for goodness sakes?"
"I'm sorry to say, but we have no more brakes."

Their cries could be heard through the streets and the heavens
As they slammed into cars by the sixes and sevens.

They rolled to a stop in front of the station,
Pried opened their eyes and hugged in elation.

"ALIVE!" Vinnie screamed, "we're alive, my friend.
I thought for a moment that this was the end."

"Au revoir, Pierre!" Vinnie shouted and ran for a seat,
And sat by a woman with really big feet.

Vinnie gasped and stared in utter surprise.
It wasn't a woman but a man in disguise.

"You're under arrest, you insufferable pet."
Vinnie looked up into the eyes of the vet.

"I laugh in the face of danger," Vinnie said.
Then pulled the vet's pants up over his head.

The vet's muffled protests couldn't be heard
While Vinnie declared the vet was a nerd.

VETERINARIAN

T.H.E.
VET

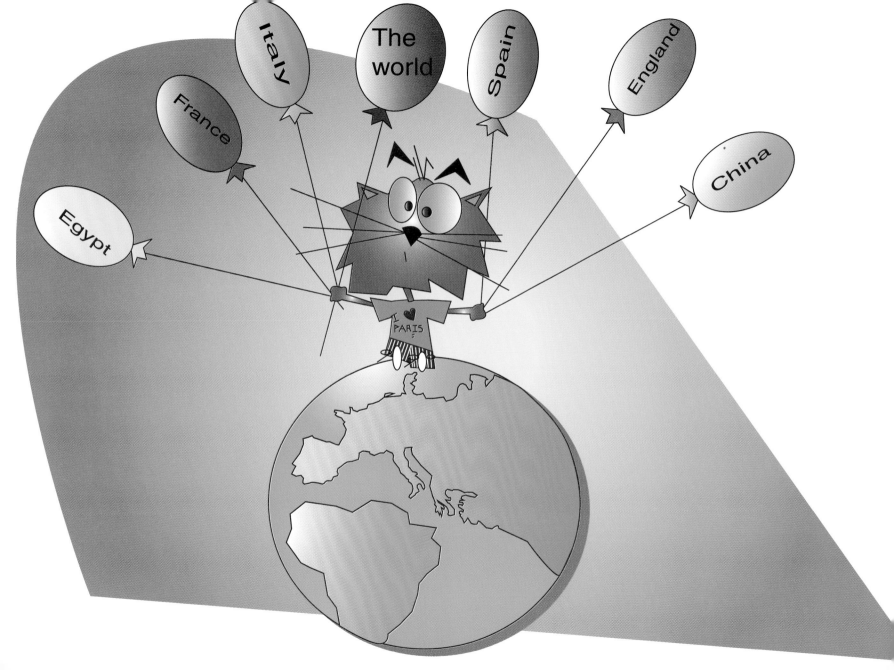

"I'm a mad crazy scamp and I live on the edge.
To travel the world is my lifelong pledge.

Nothing can stop me, not even some vet.
My dreams are much bigger than becoming a pet.

I've a mind of my own and I think for myself.
I refuse to end up like a book on a shelf."

The passengers clapped and gave a French cheer
As the conductor gave Vinnie the train to steer.

"I love French people, French bread and French fries.
French poodles aren't bad but they don't have nine lives."

From outside of the train came a horrified scream.
A woman in a wig was making a scene.

Vinnie leaned out the window and blew her a kiss.
"We'll always have Paris but it's you I'll miss."

Vinnie winked and grinned and waved goodbye.
He pulled the train whistle, "So long, sweetie pie."

Vinnie took a seat and pulled out his snack
And talked about France as they rolled down the track.

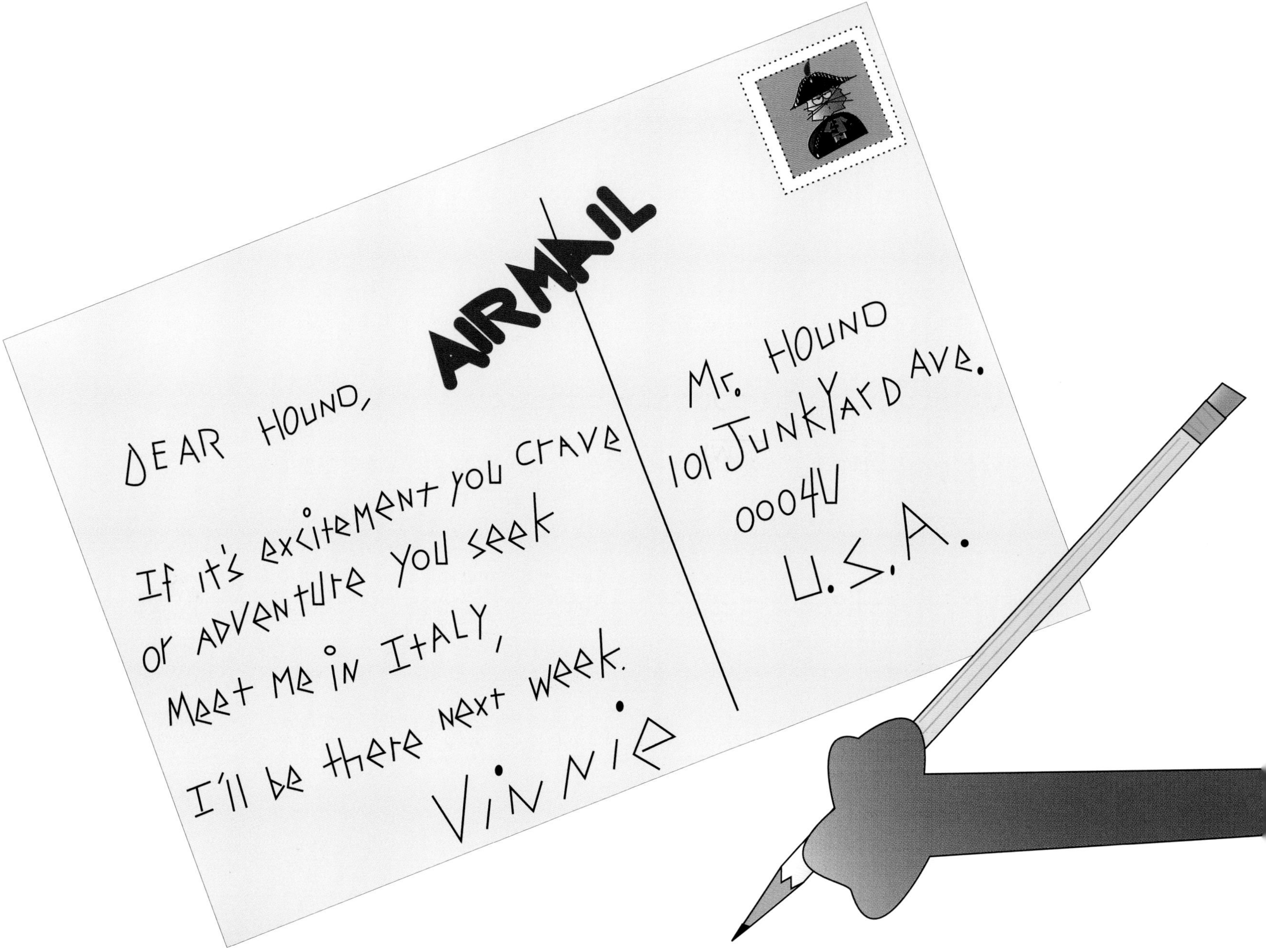
AIRMAIL
DEAR HOUND,
If it's excitement you crave
or adventure you seek
Meet me in Italy,
I'll be there next week.
Vinnie
Mr. HOUND
101 JunkYard Ave.
0004U
U.S.A.

Vinnie thought about Hound back home at the yard
And quickly wrote him a French postcard.